# Color Your
# DEGAS
## Paintings

Rendered by Marty Noble

DOVER PUBLICATIONS, INC.
Mineola, New York

# NOTE

Hilaire-Germain-Edgar Degas was born in Paris, France, on July 19, 1834. He came from a wealthy family with banking and business connections in both Italy and the United States. Degas studied law after receiving his degree from the Lycée Louis le Grand, but pursued a career in painting instead. He enrolled at the École des Beaux-Arts and also studied privately with a pupil of the painter, Ingres. He taught himself to paint by copying the Old Masters in the Louvre, and also visited art museums during his travels to Italy in the 1850s. During this time he focused on painting portraits and historical subjects.

Upon his return to Paris in 1859, Degas became friendly with fellow artists such as Whistler, Legros, Courbet, and Manet. An avid art collector as well, he began to take an interest in painting modern life subjects. Much of his art is fixated on indoor figure groups of musicians and stage performers. Subtle movements of these performers are painted in elegant, painstaking detail.

Degas is most well-known for his paintings of ballet dancers, circus performers, and horse races. These kinds of subjects afforded him the opportunity to depict fleeting moments in time and unusual angles, such as in *Miss Lala at the Cirque Fernando* (see p. 29). Akin to the view through the lens of a camera, Degas's paintings are infused with novel, unique perspectives that have come to epitomize his work.

Degas worked primarily in oils and pastels, and in the 1880s, with failing eyesight, he explored sculpture. He created a group of small bronze sculptures of dancers, bathing women, and horses, which again revealed his special ability to capture the ordinary, unobserved movements of figures. Toward the end of his life, Degas experimented with photography and also wrote poetry. He died on September 27, 1917.

All thirty of the paintings in this book are shown in full color on the inside front and back covers. Use this color scheme as a guide to create your own adaptation of a Degas or change the colors to see the effects of color and tone on each painting. Captions identify the title of the work, date of composition, medium employed, and the size of the original painting.

*Copyright*

Copyright © 2002 by Dover Publications, Inc.
All rights reserved under Pan American and International Copyright Conventions.


*Bibliographical Note*

*Color Your Own Degas Paintings* is a new work, first published by Dover Publications, Inc., in 2002.

DOVER *Pictorial Archive* SERIES

This book belongs to the Dover Pictorial Archive Series. You may use the designs and illustrations for graphics and crafts applications, free and without special permission, provided that you include no more than four in the same publication or project. (For permission for additional use, please write to Permissions Department, Dover Publications, Inc., 31 East 2nd Street, Mineola, N.Y. 11501.)

However, republication or reproduction of any illustration by any other graphic service, whether it be in a book or in any other design resource, is strictly prohibited.

*International Standard Book Number: 0-486-42376-X*

Manufactured in the United States of America
Dover Publications, Inc., 31 East 2nd Street, Mineola, N.Y. 11501

1. Dance School. 1874. Oil and tempera on canvas. 17" x 22½".

2. The Dance Foyer at the Opera. 1872. Oil on canvas. 12⅝″ x 18⅛″.

3. *A Woman with Chrysanthemums*. 1865. Oil on canvas. 29" x 36½".

4.   A Woman Having Her Hair Combed. 1886–88. Pastel on paper. 29⅛" x 23⅞".

**5.** Dancer Resting. ca. 1879. Pastel.

6. **Self-Portrait (Degas Saluant).** 1863. Oil on canvas. 36¼" x 27³⁄₁₆".

7. M. and Mme. Edmond Morbilli. 1867. Oil on canvas. 45⅝" x 35".

8. The Bellelli Family. 1860–62. Oil on canvas. 78¾" x 99⅝".

9. Hortense Valpinçon as a Child. 1869. Oil on canvas. 29¾″ x 44¾″.

10. Mme. Rene De Gas. 1872–73. Oil on canvas. 28¾" x 36¼".

11. The Cotton Market, New Orleans. 1873. Oil on canvas. 29⅛" x 36¼".

12. Women Combing Their Hair. 1875–76. Essence on paper. 12¼" x 17¾".

13. Pouting, 1873–75. Oil on canvas. 12⅝" x 18⅛".

14.   Café Concert, The Song of the Dog. 1875–77. Gouache and pastel on monotype. 22⅝" x 17⅞".

**15.   The Absinthe Drinker.** 1876. Oil on canvas. 36¼" x 26¾".

16.   The Mante Family. 1889. Pastel on paper. 35⅜" x 19⅝".

17.   The Rehearsal. 1873. Oil on canvas. 31⅞" x 25⅝".

18. The Procession (At the Race Course). 1869–72. Oil colors freely mixed with turpentine on paper. 18⅛″ x 24″.

19. Women in Front of a Café. 1877. Pastel on monotype. 16⅛″ x 23⅝″.

20.   Diego Martelli. 1879. Oil on canvas. 43¼" x 39⅜".

21.   Before the Exam (The Dancing Class). 1880. Pastel on paper. 24¾" x 18½".

22. The Millinery Shop. 1885. Oil on canvas. 38⅞" x 42⅞".

23. The Tub. 1886. Pastel on cardboard. 23⅝" x 32⅝".

24. At the Milliner's. 1882. Pastel. 29½" x 33½".

25. Mlle. Eugénie Fiocre in the Ballet "La Source". 1866. Oil on canvas. 51⅛" x 57⅞".

26.   The Tub. 1886. Pastel on paper. 27½" x 27½".

27.   Portrait of Thérèse De Gas. 1863. Oil on canvas. 35" x 26⅜".

28.   Jacques Joseph (James) Tissot. 1866–68. Oil on canvas. 59⅝" x 44".

**29.** Miss Lala at the Cirque Fernando. 1879. Oil on canvas. 46" x 30½".

30. **Six Friends of the Artist. 1885. Pastel. 45¼" x 28".**